SCIENCE Q&A

WASTE

— Melanie Ostopowich —

Weigl Publishers Inc.

Published by Weigl Publishers Inc.
350 5th Avenue, Suite 3304, PMB 6G
New York, NY 10118-0069

Website: www.weigl.com

Library of Congress Cataloging-in-Publication Data

Ostopowich, Melanie.
 Waste / Melanie Ostopowich.
     p. cm. -- (Science Q/A)
 Includes index.
 ISBN 978-1-60596-064-7 (hard cover : alk. paper) -- ISBN 978-1-60596-065-4 (soft cover : alk. paper)
 1. Refuse and refuse disposal--Miscellanea--Juvenile literature. I. Title.
 TD792.O87 2010
 363.72'8--dc22

                         2009008351

Printed in China
1 2 3 4 5 6 7 8 9 0 13 12 11 10 09

Project Coordinator
Heather C. Hudak

Design
Terry Paulhus

Photo credits
Weigl acknowledges Getty Images as its primary image supplier for this title.

Every reasonable effort has been made to trace ownership and to obtain permission to reprint copyright material. The publishers would be pleased to have any errors or omissions brought to their attention so that they may be corrected in subsequent printings.

CONTENTS

What is waste?

Everyone makes waste. Food, paper, plastic, and anything else you throw away is considered waste. Food waste, made up of rotting meat, fruits, and vegetables, makes up only 8.9 percent of garbage. Glass, paper, and plastic, which constitute a major part of waste, can be **recycled**. The average American throws away 32 pounds (12 kg) of garbage a week. That adds up to 1,664 pounds (621 kg) of garbage a year. The amount of waste in the world has a big impact on the environment. If waste is not handled properly, it can pollute the air we breathe, the water we drink, and the land on which we live. Scientists have had to come up with creative ways to handle the waste produced in the world, from designing better **landfills** to developing new methods of recycling.

Science Q&A   WASTE

What are the different types of waste?

There are two types of waste—municipal solid waste and hazardous waste.

find it quick

Learn more about hazardous waste at **www.epa.state.oh.us/dhwm/ hazardouswaste4kids.htm**.

6

Municipal solid waste is the proper name for regular garbage. This is everyday garbage, such as grass clippings or discarded food, debris from construction projects like old lumber or carpeting, and litter swept up on the street. The amount of municipal solid waste has increased steadily since World War II. New methods of using plastics led to more disposable products and packaging. In addition, a strengthening economy in the United States allowed people to buy more items and keep things for less time before replacing them. The more people began to think of their belongings as disposable, the worse the trash problem became.

Hazardous means dangerous to humans, animals, or the environment, either immediately or in the future. As surprising as it may sound, hazardous materials are used in our homes every-day. Examples of hazardous materials include gasoline, car batteries, bleach, and paint. When thrown away, these items can cause damage to people and the environment. These materials can make humans sick, release toxic fumes, or catch fire easily. Some hazardous wastes, such as radioactive materials from nuclear power plants, will remain unsafe for thousands of years. Since these items can be dangerous, there are strict rules about their disposal.

■ Radioactive wastes can remain unsafe for years, and people who handle this kind of waste have to protect themselves.

What is liquid waste?

Waste can be in liquid form as well as solid form. Liquid waste, which is usually called waste water, can come from factories, households, and rainwater that is not absorbed into the ground.

find it quick

Learn about liquid waste and more at **www.metrokc.gov/dnr/ kidsweb/haz_waste_main.htm**.

■ A septic tank is a small sewage treatment system that is common in areas with no connection to main sewage pipes.

All waste water eventually ends up in our rivers, lakes, or oceans. First, waste water must go through a cleaning process. In a city or suburban area, most waste water is treated at a sewage treatment plant. In these plants, waste water is treated to remove as much waste from it as possible. Once this is done, the treated waste water is released.

In areas that do not have a central treatment plant, households install their own treatment devices called septic tanks. Some communities, however, do not have the money or resources to keep water supplies clean. Untreated waste water can then flow into rivers, lakes, and oceans. The waste water will often contain contaminants such as gasoline, paint, pesticides, human waste from toilets, and trash. When untreated waste water is released, it can cause severe damage to water supplies.

How much garbage do we throw away?

In United States, individuals and businesses throw out more than 1 million pounds (500,000 kg) of waste per person each year.

find it quick

Make interesting objects out of recycled material at **www.make-stuff.com/recycling/index.html**.

In the 1890s, the majority of waste was ash. Homes were heated by wood and coal fires, which created ash. At the time, people rarely had garbage cans in their homes. Kitchen waste was fed to dogs and farm animals, thrown into the street or garden, or burned.

In the 1950s, the United States economy began to grow rapidly. Natural resources were seen as limitless, especially petroleum, used for powering factories and making products such as plastics. As the economy strengthened, people began to earn more money and buy more products, such as clothing, cars, and furniture. People worried less about throwing things away because it was easy and cheap to buy replacements. No one thought about recycling because they did not worry about using up natural resources, nor did they imagine that the space for storing trash would ever run out. Even today, many people still do not stop to think about what they throw away.

What is in your garbage?

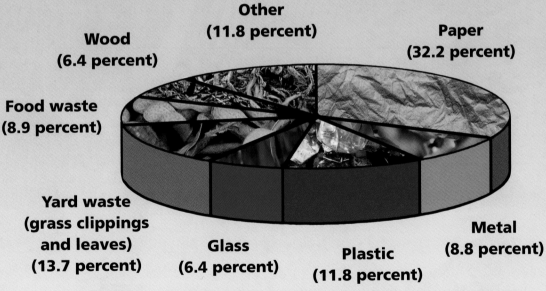

Wood (6.4 percent)

Other (11.8 percent)

Paper (32.2 percent)

Food waste (8.9 percent)

Yard waste (grass clippings and leaves) (13.7 percent)

Glass (6.4 percent)

Plastic (11.8 percent)

Metal (8.8 percent)

One Man's Trash...

A family of four throws away about 80 to 150 pounds (36 to 68 kg) of garbage each week.

Where does garbage go after we throw it away?

The United States is a large country with a huge population. The citizens create about 705, 900 tons (640, 381 tonnes) of solid trash per day. Fifty-seven percent of that trash goes into landfills, 16 percent is burned, and 27 percent is recycled.

find it quick

Learn more about what happens to trash at **www.eia.doe.gov/kids/energyfacts/saving/ recycling/solidwaste/landfiller.html**.

Garbage can end up in two different places. It can be put into a dump or in a landfill.

A dump is a place where garbage is piled in open air. Dumps cause many problems. They use up valuable land, they can harm the environment, they can attract rats, and they emit foul smell.

A landfill is a carefully designed structure built into the ground. It is located away from important environmental areas, such as water sources.

Landfills have a clay or plastic liner at the bottom to help prevent contamination of **groundwater** and soil. They also have a cap or cover on top to keep pests, such as scavenging birds, animals, and insects, from getting into the trash. Caps also keep oxygen and moisture out. This trash is compacted, or squished into spaces called cells, so the landfill can hold more

■ A landfill is a site for the disposal of waste materials. It is the oldest form of waste treatment.

waste. Landfills are not designed to break down garbage, but rather to store as much waste as possible. Landfills must comply with strict federal and state regulations to ensure that the environment does not get polluted.

Less is more

The number of landfills in the United States decreased from 8,000 in 1988 to 2,300 in 1999. However, newer landfills are much larger, so the amount of waste they can collectively hold remains the same. The number of landfills in the United States has decreased because state and local regulations are making it harder to construct new landfills.

How is a landfill made?

A landfill is more complicated than just throwing garbage into a hole in the ground.

Before a landfill can be built, scientists must study the impact it will have on the surrounding environment. They look at the soil, bedrock, and flow of water in the area planned for the landfill. They also study possible effects on the wildlife in the area. The historical value of the area must be considered as well.

Once scientists decide that a landfill can be built on a site, it is necessary to obtain permits from the local, state, and federal governments.

The basic components of a landfill are the bottom liner and the drainage system. The liner keeps the trash separate from the groundwater, and the drainage system collects the water that falls on the landfill. There is also a system installed to collect the liquid formed by water dripping through the landfill. This liquid is collected to prevent water contamination. Another machine collects methane gas, which is formed during the breakdown of the trash. In some cases, methane gas is collected and used to

generate electricity. A cover seals off the top of the landfill.

A working landfill must be opened every day as trash collectors and construction companies as well as individual citizens use landfills. When the vehicle containing the trash enters a landfill, it is weighed. The customer is charged a fee to use the landfill based on the weight of their garbage.

■ Historically, landfills have been the most common methods of organized waste disposal and remain so in many places around the world.

Take out the trash!

The highest point in Ohio is "Mount Rumpke," which is actually a mountain of trash at the Rumpke sanitary landfill.

What is the problem with landfills?

About 57 percent of garbage ends up in landfills. While this method of garbage disposal has worked well in the past, it has become less effective now.

One of the main problems with landfills is that even the biodegradable garbage inside does not break down very well. This is because landfills have airtight and watertight linings and covers. These covers keep liquid from trash, known as **leachate,** from seeping into the soil or groundwater. Unfortunately, these barriers also keep out oxygen and additional moisture needed for garbage to biodegrade.

Landfills end up storing waste, not biodegrading it. This means that landfills get full quickly, and new sites for landfills are constantly needed.

In addition, the liners at the bottom of landfills are not completely effective. Over time, they can develop cracks that allow leachate to seep through. Leachate is a poisonous substance and could leak into groundwater and eventually contaminate drinking water supplies.

Some of these substances are known to cause health problems, including cancer.

There are strict rules prohibiting toxic waste from being disposed of in regular city landfills. Even so, these landfills may still contain hazardous materials. Sometimes, toxic waste is illegally dumped in them. At other times, garbage can chemically react to produce toxins when different types are mixed with other types.

Sometimes the systems designed to keep landfills airtight and watertight can break down, which causes additional problems. Landfills have a drainage system that collects rainwater and stops it from seeping into the landfill and possibly leaking into the groundwater. Mud may clog the drainage systems, or chemicals may weaken the pipes.

Here is your challenge!

Make a miniature landfill. You will need a large container, several pieces of fruit, two small pieces of plastic, small pieces of newspaper, and soil. Place some soil at the bottom of the container. On top, keep some of the fruit and one of the plastic pieces. Take one of the small pieces of newspaper, and crumple it into a tight ball. Take another, and rip it into many small pieces. Place all of this on top of the soil. Add more soil on top of these items, covering them completely. Now, you have your own landfill, which you can observe over time.

What is leachate in groundwater?

Liquid formed from waste in landfills is called leachate. Groundwater contamination from leachate is a major concern all over the world.

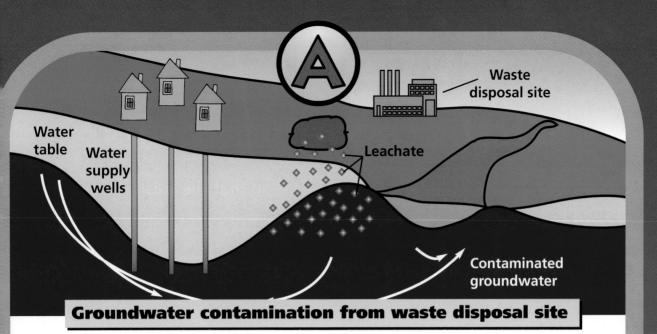

Groundwater contamination from waste disposal site

The U.S. Environmental Protection Agency (EPA) estimates that 75 percent of landfills are polluting groundwater. Groundwater is the water that lies beneath the water table. This water flows slowly but eventually emerges from underground into lakes, rivers, streams, or the ocean.

If leachate enters groundwater, it can cause a number of problems. It may even make the water unusable.

Leachate in groundwater can affect the taste and odor of the water, or it can reduce the amount of oxygen, which would affect fish and water plants. If the leachate is toxic, the water could make people and animals sick.

Municipal landfills are not supposed to have hazardous materials in them. Toxic substances may form in leachate through reactions with other substances in the garbage. The resulting toxic materials could cause cancer or birth defects.

Many of these materials have not yet been thoroughly studied by scientists. This means that the possible effects of these materials on groundwater are also unknown.

Here is your challenge!

Take two Styrofoam cups, and poke 10 small holes in the bottom of one cup with a pencil. Layer both cups with cotton, gravel, sand, and bits of grass. Put a spoonful of dirt into 1 cup (250 milliliters) of tap water. Into the other cup, pour 0.75 cup (180 ml) of the dirty water into one of the Styrofoam cups, setting the remaining 0.25 (60 ml) cup aside. Hold the cup over a glass to catch the water that comes through the holes. Will the water coming out look different than the dirty water that you set aside?

What are wet landfills?

One of the reasons a landfill is kept moist is so that the trash inside will decompose much faster.

find it
quick

Learn more about wet landfills at **www.deq.state.id.us/waste/ educ_tools/landfill_lp.pdf**.

■ A waste collection vehicle, or garbage truck, is specially designed to pick up waste and haul it to landfills and other recycling or treatment facilities.

Researchers are working on the problem of disappearing landfill space. A scientific study found that if a landfill is kept moist, the trash inside will decompose much faster. On an average, a landfill will take about 100 years to decompose. A moist landfill can decompose in just five to ten years. If a landfill is kept moist enough, bacteria will begin decomposition at a faster rate.

Leachates are a problem with many sanitary, or sealed landfills. In wet landfills, the leachates are collected and recirculated back into the garbage.

With this process, landfills would become more like treatment facilities, rather than storage facilities. A wet landfill would continually decompose old trash, creating room for new trash to be added. This would cut down on the need of more land for landfills.

How can waste be reduced?

There are two ways to reduce waste—combustion and recycling.

Burning is one way to reduce waste. The resulting ash is buried in a landfill. Burning can reduce the amount of waste sent to a landfill by 75 percent. Unfortunately, burning can release poisonous materials into the air. **Incinerators**, which are furnaces used to burn waste material, use technology to burn waste at very high temperatures in order to reduce toxic **emissions**.

Recycling prevents reusable material from ending up in a landfill or incinerator. People are becoming more aware of the importance of recycling. In 2006, 1.91 billion tons of waste were recycled. This is a major increase from the 64 million metric tons (58 million tonnes) of waste that were recycled in 1999. Currently, more than half of all aluminum products are recycled. About 45 percent of paper, such as newspaper, is recycled. About 22 percent of glass and about 36 percent of plastic are being recycled. Close to half of all recycled plastics are soda bottles. Glass and plastic are not recycled as much because these materials are expensive to process.

■ Incinerators create excess smoke and emissions.

Can we burn trash?

Although burning trash seems like a perfect solution, it does not completely solve waste problems.

Burning creates some new problems. Modern incinerators have powerful pollution control technologies. They trap ash and harmful air pollution, and prevent it from getting into the environment. Unfortunately, none of these controls are completely effective. Some smoke and ash containing dangerous material can be released into the air.

When garbage is burned, about 40 percent of the waste remains in the form of ash. Though some ash is reused in products like cement, some ends up buried in a landfill.

The ash that results from burned garbage can be toxic. This means that it can be dangerous to humans and animals. Materials such as **dioxins** and furans are formed during the burning process. These materials are known to cause cancer. Toxic ash can only be buried in landfills built to contain hazardous materials. There is always a chance that these toxic materials might get into the water supply. It is expensive to build and run incinerators.

Before modern incinerators existed, people would often burn their own trash. Today, some people still do this, especially in rural areas far away from

■ More than 13 million pounds (5,896,701 kilograms) of toxic pollutants are emitted each year from burn barrels.

dumps, landfills, or incinerators. This is a problem because there is no way to control the toxins that are released. According to the U.S. Environmental Protection Agency, backyard garbage burning, in fact, is now considered the primary source of dioxins in the air. Due to the many problems with burning trash, incineration is not likely to be the cure for our garbage problems. Other methods will have to be explored.

Is there waste in the air?

Air pollution is a major concern. There are many sources of air pollution, including factories and smoke from incinerators.

Vehicles such as cars, buses, and trucks also cause air pollution. More than 245 million vehicles are registered in the United States.

Emissions from vehicles, which are materials released into the air when car engines burn fuel, not only affect air quality but also add to the greenhouse effect, also known as global warming. Vehicles can also release toxic materials into the air, some of which are known to cause cancer.

Scientists and engineers have been designing vehicles that use different sources of fuel. These new vehicles run on electricity and natural gas, resulting in much lower emissions. Some of these vehicles are in the market.

Other companies are producing cleaner gas, which also results in lower emissions. In addition, some states are enforcing tougher emission standards, which means that people are only allowed to drive cars that produce low emissions.

What are greenhouse gases?

Component	Effect
Carbon monoxide	Poisonous gas
Particulate (soot)	Contains chemicals known to cause cancer
Lead	Poisonous
Greenhouse gases, including:	
• Carbon dioxide	Major cause of global warming
• Nitrogen oxides	Contribute to acid rain and smog; cause breathing problems
• Hydrocarbons	Contribute to smog; have an unpleasant smell
• Sulfur oxides	Contribute to acid rain

HYBRID SYNERGY DRIVE

Roadhouse Blues

It would take 20 new cars to generate the same amount of air pollution as one car from the mid-1960s. Unfortunately, the distance people drive every day has increased since the 1960s, so overall air pollution has become worse instead of better.

Is land being wasted?

Increased land development creates a number of problems. These include increased waste production, traffic congestion, air pollution, and increased energy use.

As the population of the United States grows, so does the size of cities and towns. This is a phenomenon known as urban sprawl. In a short span of time, millions of acres of land in the United States are being converted into houses, malls, and parking lots. The rate of development is very high compared to what it was more than a decade ago.

One of the problems with increasing development is that it seems to be happening at a faster rate than the population is growing. For example, in New York between 1970 and 1990, the population grew by only about 5 percent, but land use increased by 61 percent. At this rate, there will not be any land left.

Another concern about land development is the loss of farmland and habitat for native animals. Long-term habitat loss is one of the main reasons that animal species are becoming extinct. Without a place to live, an animal cannot survive.

■ Deforestation is the destruction of large areas of forest cover for use as pasture, urban use, or landfills.

Farewell Forests

In the United States, more than 34 million acres (13 million hectares) of open space were lost to development between 1982 and 2001. This is equal to about 6,000 acres (2,428 ha) per day and 4 acres (1.6) a minute. Of this loss, more than 10 million acres (4 million ha) were in forests.

What does biodegradable mean?

When a material is biodegradable, it means that living things can break it down.

find it quick

Learn more about biodegradable material at **http://library.thinkquest.org/6076/New% 20Pages/KidsDoRecPileBio.html**.

Under the right conditions, material can be broken down into simple **compounds**, such as carbon dioxide and water. The process of decay releases these compounds back into the environment so that they can be used again.

Decay may seem a little unappealing, and people often try to stop it from happening. Putting grass clippings into a plastic bag and sending it to a landfill, rather than **composting** it, is an example of this attitude toward waste.

If nothing were recycled, the nutrients and resources in the world would be used up entirely.

■ Many objects, especially those made of plastic, are not biodegradable.

Many things are needed for a material to biodegrade. Bacteria and other simple organisms in soil eat and digest biodegradable material. Insects and worms do the same thing, breaking down materials. Oxygen and moisture are also usually needed, as well as the right temperature.

Different materials break down at different rates. How long a material takes to decompose depends on its content.

Does packaging make unnecessary waste?

When you buy an item at the store, it often comes wrapped up in plastic, paper, cardboard, or glass.

When you open the package and take out the item, what happens to the packaging? Does the packaging get used, recycled, or thrown away?

In the United States, packaging materials make up one-third of all waste. Packaging materials include not only fast-food boxes, plastic bags, and cans but also wooden pallets, cardboard cartons, plastic wraps, and crates, all of which protect the products before they get to store shelves.

Products use packaging for a number of reasons. It helps to reduce theft and tampering, prevents products from breaking, and keeps food items fresh. It can make products easier to handle by adding features like handles or spouts. Finally, packaging provides a surface for written information about the product.

Packaging has important uses. Still, the amount of packaging being used today is a problem. Some manufacturers have reduced the amount of packaging they use for their products. They are using thinner, lighter, and fewer plastics, metals, and paper. Some have also started to use biodegradable packing peanuts made from cornstarch for shipping purposes rather than polystyrene plastic.

Doing this cuts down on the amount of garbage, saves money on materials, and reduces shipping costs. People can also help reduce the amount of packaging waste by buying products that have little or no packaging.

■ Packing peanuts are a common material used to prevent damage to fragile objects during shipping.

Is it better to use paper bags or plastic bags?

At the grocery store, people are often asked if they want paper or plastic bags to hold their groceries. Some people choose paper. Others choose plastic. These people may believe one type of bag is better for the environment or produces less waste.

find it quick

Learn more about conserving energy by recycling plastic at **www.eia.doe.gov/kids/energyfacts/saving/recycling/solidwaste/plastics.html**.

Many people choose paper over plastic bags at the grocery store because paper bags are easier to recycle. Paper and plastic both have advantages and disadvantages, but it is difficult to determine if one is actually better than the other. The problem with plastic is that it is not really biodegradable.

Paper is more commonly accepted in recycling programs. There are seven different types of plastics used in packaging. Most U.S. states require plastics to have identification codes so they can be easily identified and separated according to their thickness.

Plastic was once thought of as a wonder-material. It is cheap, versatile, and disposable. But it is non-biodegradable and takes 1,000 years or more to degrade, which causes a great deal of damage to the environment.

Plastic can be recycled, but only through a complicated process. With so many different types, plastic must be sorted before it is recycled. In addition, plastic can only be recycled once or twice because the quality of the plastic decreases each time.

Paper makes up about 40 to 50 percent of waste in landfills. However, over time, paper should break down and disappear. Paper is easily recycled and can be reused many times before the fibers in the paper become unusable.

These advantages may make paper seem like a better choice than plastic, but there are other factors to consider. The lack of oxygen and moisture in most landfills means nothing really biodegrades—not even paper.

Plastic takes up very little space in landfills. Scientists have now invented biodegradable plastics that decompose in the natural environment.

Plastic Pile

Americans use four million plastic bottles every hour. Only one out of four bottles is recycled after use.

What are the three Rs?

The three Rs stand for reduce, reuse, and recycle.

find it quick

Learn about recycling at
http://www.kidsrecycle.org.

■ Recycling involves processing used materials into new products to prevent waste and reduce the use of fresh materials.

Reducing waste means that less garbage will be thrown away and landfills will take longer to fill up. There are many ways to cut down on waste. When shopping, you can buy products that are made to last or are reusable. Also, choosing products with less packaging means that less trash will be thrown away.

Similar to reducing waste, reusing products means that less waste will end up in a landfill. If it is impossible to reuse an item, it does not have to be thrown away. Instead, the item can be given away or sold to allow someone else to use it. Also, if something is broken, it may be possible to mend it rather than throwing it away.

Recycling turns potential waste into new products. Recycling not only saves items from ending up in a landfill or incinerator, it also helps the environment by preventing new resources from being used to make the same products. For example, recycling paper saves trees from being cut down. Also, recycling tin cans means that new metals will not have to be mined. This saves energy and reduces the pollution caused by mining activities.

There are easy ways to reduce, reuse, and recycle. Use cloth napkins or towels instead of paper. Refill, reuse, or recycle bottles. Donate things that you no longer use to charities. Use refillable pens and reusable pencils. Use empty jars to hold items such as leftover food. Use rechargeable batteries. Use cloth bags at the grocery store rather than paper or plastic. Use grass clippings to make compost rather than throwing them away.

What can be recycled?

Many everyday items can be recycled. If an effort were made to recycle all of these items, much less waste would end up in landfills or incinerators. Recycling also saves energy and resources, and reduces air and water pollution.

find it quick

Learn more about the U.S. Environmental Protection Agency Garbage and Recycling program at **www.epa.gov/kids/garbage.htm**.

Manufacturing a can from recycled aluminum reduces air and water pollution by more than 95 percent compared to manufacturing a can from raw materials. Recycling one aluminum can saves enough energy to run a television for three hours. Enough aluminum is thrown away to rebuild the entire U.S. commercial airline fleet four times a year.

Creating a glass bottle from recycled glass reduces air pollution by 20 percent and water pollution by 50 percent compared to manufacturing glass from raw materials. By recycling one glass jar, enough energy is saved to light a 100-watt bulb for four hours. Glass can be recycled many times.

Recycled paper reduces air and water pollution by 55 percent compared to manufacturing paper from new wood. Currently, enough paper is thrown away every year to build a 12-foot (4-m) wall from New York to California.

The United States uses 14 billion pounds (6.4 billion kg) of plastics each year, but only about 5 percent is recycled. The recycled plastics are used to make fibers, containers, bottles, pipes, lawn and garden products, and car parts.

Aluminum, which is used to make cans, is highly recyclable.

Each year, recycling steel saves enough energy to supply electricity to 18 million homes for one year. It also reduces the mining of resources, such as iron ore, coal, and limestone. Currently, the amount of iron and steel thrown away could be used to supply the nation's automakers continually.

Why are people recycling less?

People are now recycling less than they did in the 1990s. For the first time in 20 years, Americans are throwing away more aluminum cans than they recycle.

There are several possible reasons for this decline in recycling. Many cities have curbside pickup of recycling materials. Programs like this cost money, and if a city is having financial problems, the program may be stopped. If this happens, less waste is recycled because individuals are less likely to drop off recyclables at recycling centers.

The price of aluminum scrap metal has also dropped because of decreased demand for aluminum products. Recycling aluminum cans provides less money than it once did.

In addition, the cost of making products from recycled materials is higher than the cost of making new products. Before recyclable material can be reused, it must be sorted, cleaned, and processed. Companies that process recyclables must pay people to do this extra work. They then charge higher prices to other companies that want to buy recycled materials for use in their own products. The result is that many companies are not willing to use recycled materials at all.

Despite the costs, recycling has many benefits. It takes a large amount of energy to make aluminum. Producing a soda can from recycled aluminum uses 96 percent less energy and produces 95 percent less air pollution and 97 percent less water pollution than manufacturing a new can.

The long-term cost savings and advantages make recycling good for the environment and for people. However, until the price of recycled materials goes down, or laws are passed requiring companies to use these materials, a major improvement in the amount of recycling performed in the United States is unlikely.

Steady Decline

In 2007, 53.8 percent of the aluminum cans sold in the United States were recycled. In 1991, 60 percent were recycled.

Science Q&A **Q** WASTE

What is composting?

Composting is also a form of recycling and a way to reduce the amount of waste in landfills.

find it quick

Learn more about composting at **www.sustainable.tamu.edu/ slidesets/kidscompost/cover.html.**

Composting is the controlled decomposition and decay of organic matter. Organic matter includes food waste, such as fruit and vegetable peels, leftovers, and eggshells. It also includes yard waste, such as grass clippings, leaves, and small weeds. This organic mixture decomposes into a soil-like material. Composting is nature's way of recycling.

Composting keeps organic waste out of landfills, where it would never break down. Composting ensures that these materials decompose and become useful to the environment.

Compost is used in flower and vegetable gardens and landscaping. It can be added to soil as a fertilizer to make flowers and vegetables grow well. Compost also reduces the need for chemical fertilizers and pesticides. Fertilizers and pesticides can be harmful to the environment, causing toxic materials to seep into the ground and even the water supply. Composting has been known to prevent disease in plants, increase helpful soil organisms, such as worms, and protect soil from being washed away by rain or blown away by wind.

Here is your challenge!

Place kitchen waste into a composting container, such as a wooden box. Add kitchen waste and other organic material. Spread soil over the top of the compost pile. This layer contains the microorganisms needed to make the compost and keeps the surface moist. Allow the compost pile to "bake" in a sunny area. It should heat up quickly. Stir the pile with a shovel occasionally to speed up the process of decay. As composting occurs, the pile should begin to settle. If you mix and turn it every week, your compost will be ready for use in one or two months. If not, it could take up to 12 months.

Waste Careers

Scientist

As garbage increases each year, many scientists are dedicated to finding other methods of waste disposal. Earlier, garbage was not a problem because it was biodegradable and would disappear with time. New inventions introduced materials that do not disappear quickly. An aluminum can takes 200 to 500 years to break down. A Styrofoam cup will never break down. Nonbiodegradable trash became a problem with growing populations. People began running out of places to dispose their trash. To solve this, scientists are trying to develop new ways to get rid of garbage and trying to find new and better ways to recycle items, so people will not need to throw away as much as they currently do.

Environmental Engineer

An environmental engineer designs and maintains pollution control techniques, designs landfills, and develops systems to reverse damage done to the environment. An environmental engineer's work may involve solid waste disposal, water and air pollution control, or controlling hazardous wastes. In this job, you might work with people from all levels of government, as well as community groups and other scientists and engineers. Environmental engineers usually have a degree in engineering from a university or college. Working as a volunteer in your city's environmental office would be a great way to see if this type of career is for you.

find it quick

Learn more about waste careers at **http://www.wm.com/ wm/careers/overview.asp**.

Young scientists at work

Test your knowledge of waste with these questions and activities. You can probably answer the questions using this book, your own experiences, and your common sense.

FACT

Different types of garbage should be dealt with in different ways.

TEST

Look at the four photos of different types of garbage. Then, look at the three recycling methods of getting rid of garbage. Match each type of garbage to the best method of disposal.

A. Recycling center
B. Compost
C. Hazardous waste landfill

Answers

A. Newspaper, glass bottles, tin cans—go to a recycling center.
B. Grass clippings and leftover food—make into compost.
C. Hazardous materials (bleach, paint, etc.)—hazardous waste landfill.

FACT

Many items that are thrown away are actually recyclable.

TEST

Which of the following items are recyclable?

Glass bottles, plastic containers, newspapers, tin cans, disposable diapers, leftover food, grass clippings, metal.

Answers

Glass, plastics, newspapers, tin cans, and metal can all be recycled. Disposable diapers are not commonly recyclable. While leftover food and grass clippings cannot be recycled, they can be composted and added to soil.

Take a science survey

Everybody creates garbage. Many people also recycle, reuse, and reduce their waste. Does your family recycle its garbage? Take this survey home to learn about your family's recycling habits.

What are your answers?

1. Which of the following items go into your garbage?

   cans, glass bottles, paper, styrofoam, newspapers, grocery bags, batteries, clothing, disposable diapers

2. Which of these items are recyclable?

3. Does your town or city have a place to recycle any of these items?

4. Where does your garbage go when it leaves your house?

5. How does reusing things help the environment?

SURVEY RESULTS

Most of the items listed in question 1 are recyclable. When people throw away garbage, it usually ends up in a landfill. Landfill space is becoming scarce. Every time people throw something away, they also throw away the energy, money, raw materials, and water it took to make it. Recycling saves these items from ending up in a landfill and allows materials in them to be reused.

46

Fast Facts

The United States has 6 percent of the world's population and creates 50 percent of the world's garbage.

Glass bottles will last for up to one million years if not recycled.

Every day, U.S. businesses use enough paper to circle Earth twenty times.

The first aluminum recycling plant opened in Chicago in 1904.

About 220 tons (200 tonnes) of computers and other electronic waste are dumped in landfills and incinerators every year in the United States.

If all Americans recycled just their Sunday paper, it would save an entire forest of 500,000 trees each week.

In the 1900s, pigs were used to get rid of garbage in several cities. One expert reported that 75 pigs could eat 1 ton (0.9 tonnes) of garbage per day.

Not only does smoking cause lung cancer, it is also bad for the environment. Cigarette butts will last for one to five years before they decompose.

Americans receive about 52 billion pieces of advertising in their mailboxes every year.

When 1 ton (0.9 tonnes) of paper is recycled, seventeen trees are saved.

Glossary

composting: breaking down organic materials, such as yard, garden, and kitchen wastes, to produce a rich, soil-like mixture

compounds: a whole formed by a union of two or more elements or parts

dioxins: toxic substances formed when materials are burned

emissions: substances that are released into the air

groundwater: water beneath the earth's surface between soil and deep layers of rock. This water supplies springs and wells, and may be used as drinking water

incinerators: furnaces or other devices used for burning waste

landfills: systems of garbage disposal in which waste is buried between layers of earth

leachate: water that leaks through a dump or landfill, picking up pollutants along the way

recycled: used again

Index